anta,
a
rmor,
a
brother
o doesn't
cry, a shield,

Visit us on the Web!
randomhousekids.com
Babymouse.com

Educators and librarians, for a variety of teaching tools,
visit us at RHTeachersLibrarians.com

Library of Congress Cataloging-in-Publication Data is available upon request.

ISBN 978-1-101-93743-3 (trade) — ISBN 978-1-101-93744-0 (lib. bdg.) —
ISBN 978-1-101-93745-7 (ebook)

Book design by John Sazaklis

MANUFACTURED IN CHINA

10 9 8 7 6 5 4 3 2 1

First Edition

Random House Children's Books supports the First Amendment
and celebrates the right to read.

For Missy
—J.L.H.

For Nathan
—M.H.

JENNIFER L. HOLM & MATTHEW HOLM

LiTTLE
BABYMOUSE
and the
Christmas Cupcakes

RANDOM HOUSE 🏠 NEW YORK

It was Christmas Eve.

And Babymouse was putting out cookies for Santa.

Well, if you want to earn that armor, you should think about baking Santa some more cookies.

PARFAITS!

ICED CAKE!

PIE!

TART!

TUNA CASSEROLE!

Tuna casserole?

CRACK!

OOPS! MISSED.

SPLAT!

I thought you weren't supposed to touch them, Babymouse.

Oh, Babymouse.

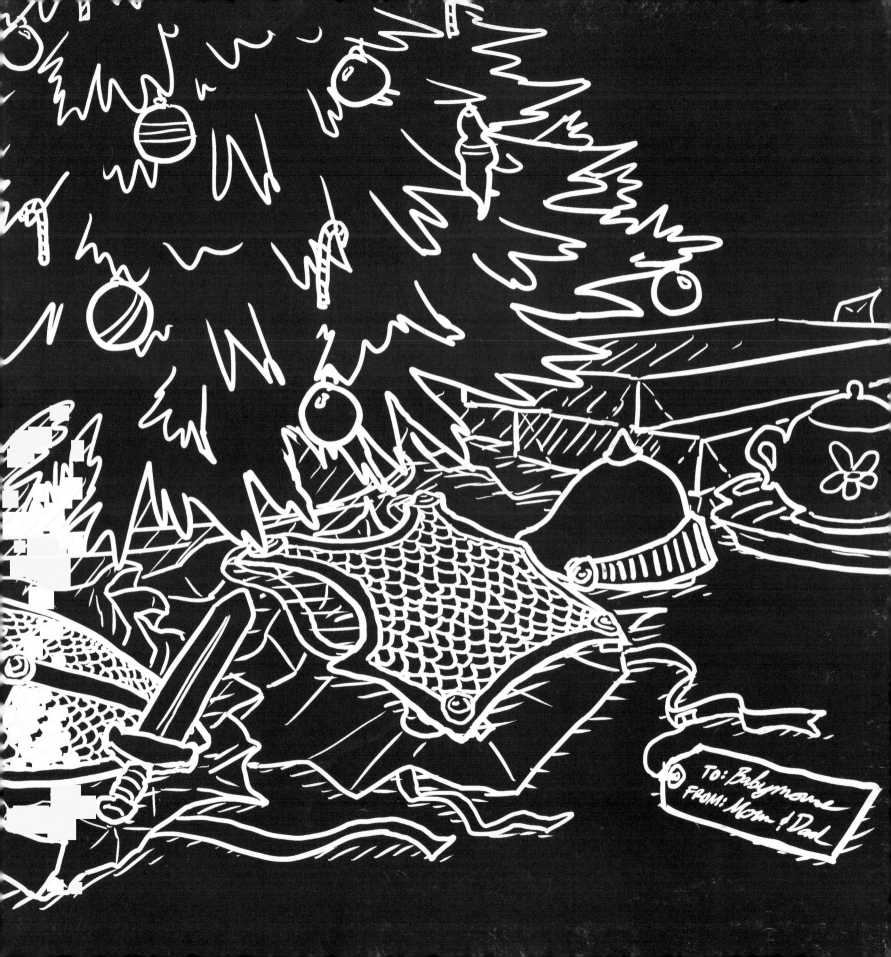